KNIGHTS OF RIGHT

Also by M'Lin Rowley

Knights of Right, book 1: *The Falcon Shield*

Illustrations by Michael Walton

©2009 Melissa Rowley

Visit us at ShadowMountain.com

Library of Congress Cataloging-in-Publication Data
Rowley, M'Lin.
  The silver coat / M'Lin Rowley.
    p.   cm. — (Knights of right ; bk. 2)
    Summary: Brothers Joseph, twelve, and Ben, ten, return to the castle
of King Arthur, who sends them on a second quest against a real-life
enemy, guided by signs brought by the falcon, True Heart.
    ISBN 978-1-60641-104-9 (paperbound : alk. paper)
    [1. Knights and knighthood—Fiction.   2. Conduct of life—Fiction.
3. Honesty—Fiction.   4. Brothers—Fiction.   5. Time travel—Fiction.   6. Arthur,
King—Fiction.   7. Kings, queens, rulers, etc.—Fiction.
I. Title.
  PZ7.R79834Sil 2009
  [Fic]—dc22
                                                                    2009009633

Printed in the United States of America
Malloy Lithographing Incorporated, Ann Arbor, MI

10   9   8   7   6   5   4   3

KNIGHTS OF RIGHT

BOOK 2
THE SILVER COAT

M'LIN ROWLEY

SHADOW
MOUNTAIN

1

THE FALCON'S SIGNAL

Twelve-year-old Joseph, returning from soccer practice, headed straight for the back-yard. Dad and ten-year-old Ben were already there, hammers in their hands. Planks of wood lay at their feet, and a page of plans sat forgotten on the grass behind them.

"What do you think, Joseph?" Ben asked when he saw his older brother on the porch. "Should we give the birdhouse a pointed roof or make the top flat?"

"Give it a pointed roof, totally! T. H. deserves better than a box for a house."

1

The falcon they were discussing, True Heart (T. H. for short), rested on the branch of the tree nearby. The tree house they had built earlier this summer was near the fence that separated their yard from the woods. That was where their first amazing adventure had happened only a few weeks before.

"Has T. H. tried to get you into the woods since you got home from school?" Joseph whispered to Ben when Dad went to the back porch to grab more nails. Ben shook his head and they both looked up at the bird.

"King Arthur said T. H. would lead us to the castle when it was time for the next quest, didn't he?" Ben asked, frowning. "Why hasn't T. H. done anything? Why is it taking so long?"

Joseph shrugged, and the boys stopped talking as Dad came back over.

"Let's build this roof!" Dad cheered. They took turns nailing the roof together and then stepped back to admire the job they'd done.

"Now T. H. will have somewhere to sleep until his real owner finds him," Dad smiled.

Ben and Joseph shared a knowing look. The flyers that their babysitter, Sam, had made for them about a "tame falcon" would never be answered, because True Heart belonged to King Arthur.

The boys had met King Arthur when they'd gone exploring in the woods behind their house. His castle had saved them from the evil Black Knight who had chased them through the forest. King Arthur had challenged them to become knights in training for the Round Table, and now they had to complete certain quests as part of their training. Ben and Joseph and Sam had earned shields after the first quest. Now the boys were anxiously waiting for True Heart to lead them back to the castle for their next quest.

"Thanks for helping us make T. H.'s house, Dad!" Ben said.

"No problemo! I'm glad I was able to get off early the last few days. But I'm afraid my schedule's getting busy again." The boys grumbled their complaints, and Dad ruffled their hair.

"Do you always have to work late? Sam's cool, but she can't help us build stuff or . . ." Ben's sentence trailed off into silence. He and Joseph looked at Dad hopefully for his answer.

"Sorry, boys. I have to bring home the bacon," Dad said.

Just then Mom called to them from the doorway, a plate of something in her hands. "Great work, guys! I bet T. H. will love it! You finished just in time. Dinner will be ready in half an hour."

At that moment True Heart sailed down and snatched a piece of bacon from the plate, carrying his prize to Ben's shoulder.

Ben, Joseph, and Dad cracked up as Mom stamped her foot in frustration. "That bird— this bacon is for dinner! How am I supposed to make BLTs if your bird eats all the bacon?"

"Dad brings home the bacon, and T. H. eats it," Ben said, and the boys laughed even harder. Mom shook her head as Dad followed her back into the house.

True Heart fluttered off Ben's shoulder and landed on the roof of his new house. He gave a little screech and then launched up into the air, only to land on the fence. Then he screeched again and flew a short distance to the first tree in the woods.

"It's the sign!" Joseph gasped. He and Ben smiled at each other and ran to the tree house to grab their shields. Then they climbed the fence.

2

THE BLACK HORSE

When they were in the woods, Ben danced in a circle gleefully.

"Let's go see King Arthur! Oh, yeah! Woo-hoo! Ride 'em, cowboy! Holy Toledo! Oh, mama!" Ben shouted all kinds of odd stuff to show how excited he was.

Joseph put a hand on Ben's shoulder to quiet him; he heard a faint noise coming from deeper in the woods and put a finger to his lips. "Did you hear that? It sounds like . . . pounding."

Both boys held still and tried to hear it.

Joseph crouched down on all fours and put his ear to the ground. He'd seen that in a movie once.

"It's horse hooves!" Joseph said delightedly, happy he'd been the one to figure it out. The boys smiled, until they considered who might be riding a horse in the woods behind their house.

"What if it's the Black Knight?" Ben gasped.

Joseph pulled him over to a fallen log, and they ducked behind it. Seconds later the Black Knight stormed past on a gleaming black horse with hooves the size of plates. His speed sent leaves flying into the air. Joseph covered his face with his shield because of all the dust the horse kicked up.

"That was a close one!" Ben said as he

began breathing. He hadn't realized he'd been holding his breath.

"You can say that again." Joseph nodded as he stood up.

"That was a close one!" Ben repeated.

Joseph rolled his eyes, and Ben grinned.

"Do you think he saw us?" Joseph asked.

"I don't think so, or he would still be here trying to kill us," Ben answered in a completely serious voice.

Joseph would have thought Ben was exaggerating—as usual—if he didn't know better. The Black Knight *had* tried to kill them during their last adventure. At least now they had their shields and T. H. But they still had to be careful.

"I think we can get to the castle before he

comes back, but we'd better hurry," Joseph decided.

True Heart led the boys through the woods to the old castle. Its crumbling walls looked mysterious but welcoming at the same time. Joseph was always surprised that the huge building hadn't been seen by anyone, but maybe it was like their shields—invisible to everyone but them.

The big wooden drawbridge was being lowered slowly when they approached, just as it had been the two other times they'd been there. They still couldn't see who was letting it down, but once inside, they walked through the door at the end of the courtyard to the throne room.

There King Arthur sat on his throne, a large smile on his face. His hunting dog was

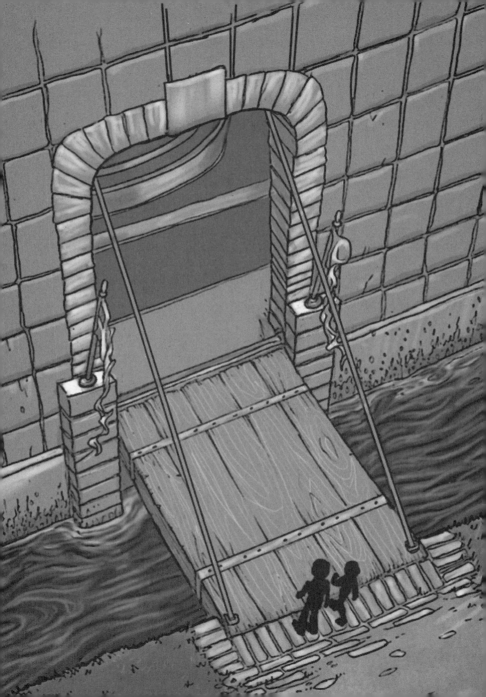

by his feet. It sat there, panting happily, watching the boys with intelligent eyes. Joseph waved at it, and the dog gave him a cheerful bark.

"Young Benjamin! Young Joseph! I am so glad to see you! Thank you for coming!" King Arthur smiled at them.

"Guess what!" Ben said excitedly. He didn't wait for an answer. "Sam got a shield too! But Sam wasn't at our house today when T. H. gave the sign, and even if she was at our house she would be babysitting Katie, and Katie can't come out to the forest." The words poured out in a huge rush.

King Arthur smiled. "Lady Samantha can be of assistance to our cause exactly where she is. Tell her I am honored she would join us."

"So much has happened, Your Majesty!" Joseph chimed in. "When we left the castle last time, the Black Knight attacked us. But Ben's shield saved us! Look!"

Ben held up his shield and pointed to the dent in it where the arrow had hit.

"Do you think we'll need our shields when we aren't in the woods?" Joseph asked.

"They'll make great snowboards this winter!" Ben laughed.

Joseph elbowed him and gave him a big brother look that said "Cut it out."

"I have never seen this sport of snowboarding. Perhaps someday you could teach me," King Arthur suggested politely.

"I can't wait to see you snowboard in your flowing royal robes! That'd be classic!" Ben laughed.

King Arthur smiled cheerfully too, not the least insulted.

"Ben, that was rude," Joseph whispered to his brother harshly. "I'm sure you'd be a great snowboarder, Your Majesty," he said loudly.

"No, Ben is right. I would look quite ridiculous. I had better stick to storytelling," King Arthur said.

Ben and Joseph scrambled to get a good seat at the king's feet, ready for another story. The last time King Arthur had told them a story, it had to do with their quest. Joseph hoped that if he listened closer this time, he would be able to tell what his new quest was.

3

THE FOOLISH KNIGHT AND THE DRAGON

"In my kingdom was a foolish knight who took great pleasure in bragging to his friends and trying to sound important and brave. One day he found several dragon scales in the woods. Stringing the scales into a necklace, he pretended to have defeated the dragons and stolen the scales off their dead bodies." King Arthur leaned back, folded his arms, and looked at the ceiling, as if lost in the memory.

Joseph made a disgusted face at the mention of taking the scales off the bodies, but

Ben nodded with a smile and mouthed, "Cool."

"During one long, hard winter, this foolish man sold the dragon scales to make some money, and his tales about killing many dragons spread far and wide. Perhaps a dragon heard these stories and became angry. Perhaps the foolish man became greedy for more dragons' scales and tried to steal them from a dragon's cave. Whatever the reason, the poor man disappeared in the spring and was never heard from again.

"A noble knight from the Round Table considered this man his friend and went in search of him. His search led him to the cave of the dragon Mintara. The knight respectfully stood at the entrance of the cave and called out to the dragon, asking if she knew the missing man. Mintara answered, 'I have killed your terrible dragon fighter. It was far too easy, and he tasted weak and pitiful to me.'

"Saddened by his friend's death, the knight asked for the shield of the foolish knight to take back to his family. Mintara agreed to let the knight enter her cave if he promised to take nothing but the shield. He gave his word. The dragon left her treasure pile and crawled out of the cave. But she expected the knight to steal her treasure, so she waited for him to appear. After hours of searching through the dragon's treasure, the knight found the shield and appeared at the mouth of the cave. Mintara scorched the cave entrance with a burst of deadly fire."

"But that's not fair," said Joseph. "What happened to the knight?"

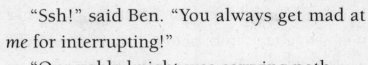

"Ssh!" said Ben. "You always get mad at
me for interrupting!"

"Our noble knight was carrying nothing but the shield," the king continued,
"which he held in front of him. Thus,
he was protected. Angry that she

had not killed the knight, Mintara spread her wings to attack from above, just as the knight picked up his lance and threw it at her. It found its mark in her heart, and the great dragon Mintara died in front of her own cave."

"That is sad!" Ben frowned.

"It's not sad! The first knight was stupid. That's why King Arthur called him a 'foolish man.' In a way, he deserved to die," Joseph explained impatiently.

"I wasn't talking about that. It's sad that the dragon died," Ben retorted.

"It is a sad thing when anyone dies. Do not feel joy over the foolish man's death, young Joseph. It is heartbreaking that he died without reason when he could have lived. He died before he had done any good with his life. That is one of the reasons I am so proud of you boys. You are becoming finer young men as you complete each quest. That may seem like a small thing, but you are making the world a better place for us all.

"As you begin your next quest, consider this question. Did the knight take Mintara's treasure after her death? I will want to know your answer when you return." King Arthur smiled affectionately as the boys stood to go.

"We'll think about it, Your Majesty. See you later! Thanks for the cool story! It was so cool!" Ben called back. The boys walked out of the throne room into the bright courtyard.

"Nice descriptions—very original. *Cool* and *cool*," Joseph teased as the drawbridge was let down by an unseen someone. They ran out to the forest.

"I bet you couldn't do better," Ben challenged as they hid behind a tree. They were waiting for True Heart's signal that it was safe. Finally the falcon called to them with a loud shriek, and they left the safety of the tree.

"Let me see. It was an amazing, superb, fantastic, wonderful, terrific, brilliant, inspired, and magnificent story," Joseph said.

"Sometimes I wish I were a nerd too," Ben sighed, but a mischievous grin appeared on his face. "Only sometimes. Then I remember how much cooler I am than you, and I'm cool with not being a nerd."

"Oh, man! You are going to regret calling me a nerd, Mr. Cool-is-the-only-word-I-know!"

Joseph laughed, and Ben bolted into the forest with Joseph hot on his tail.

4

A CLUE THAT RATTLES

Joseph stopped chasing Ben when he realized he couldn't see True Heart anymore. He was afraid to call the falcon because he didn't want to attract the Black Knight's attention. Ben skidded to a stop and spun around, nervously scanning the trees.

"Do you think we got lost, or did T. H.?" Ben asked anxiously. Joseph wanted to act the part of the brave older brother, but it wasn't good to be lost in the forest with the Black Knight around.

True Heart suddenly swooped down and

landed on a branch above them. Clutched tightly in his beak was an angry, writhing rattlesnake. With bared fangs and rattles buzzing, the snake was terrifying. The boys took a step or two backwards.

"Where in the world did you get that, T. H.?" Joseph gasped.

"It's so cool!" Ben's eyes were glued to the snake. Joseph shook his head and smiled at his brother's fascination.

"It's not cool. It's dangerous. Do you think it's the first clue?" Joseph asked.

"I don't know, but here's what we're going to do. We'll put the rattlesnake in the middle of the road and wait for the Black Knight to come. Then when the rattlesnake bites his horse and the horse goes down, we'll pounce on the Black Knight with our mighty skills!"

Ben demonstrated his mighty skills by throwing some punches in the direction of a gray squirrel. The squirrel chattered at him angrily and scampered up a tree.

"Yeah, right! Even without his horse we still can't take him. He's a pro, and we're just kids," Joseph argued.

"King Arthur always says just because we're kids doesn't mean we can't do stuff," Ben answered. He started walking along the path bent over, scanning the ground.

"What in the world are you doing? Do you realize you look absolutely ridiculous?" Joseph tried hard not to laugh at his brother.

"I'm looking for horse dung. If we can find that, then we'll know which path the horse usually takes." Ben kept walking, hunched over with his knees slightly bent.

Joseph looked up to make sure True Heart was still okay. The falcon was fine. The snake's tongue slithered angrily in and out of its mouth as it hissed at Joseph.

"The Black Knight has all kinds of weapons, and all we have is our shields, Ben. I think you should give up this crazy dung search, and we'll figure out the clue later," Joseph urged.

Ben grumbled, but he followed Joseph and True Heart back to the fence. Mom was just calling them for dinner as Ben watched the falcon kill the snake with his claws and start to eat it.

"That's so cool," he mused.

5

A CLUE THAT COULDN'T TALK

The next day the boys met in the tree house right after school. Joseph pulled out their box of plastic building blocks, and soon they were both immersed in a world of their own creation. Ben proudly finished a cube and looked over to see Joseph adding the mast to an amazing pirate ship. Ben's jaw dropped as he looked from his little box to the elaborate ship. He sheepishly took his cube apart before Joseph could see it. Joseph looked over a few seconds later.

"What are you going to make?" he asked.

Ben shrugged. "I'm deciding between a space shuttle and a castle."

"Wow! You're really good if you can do it just by looking at the pieces. I had to use the instructions," Joseph said, holding up a little booklet.

"Oh! Do you have an instruction book I could borrow?" Ben asked, blushing, and the two brothers laughed.

True Heart landed on the windowsill and flung something into the room. It hit the floor with a squish.

"Eww! What is that?" Joseph asked. Ben scooted over and poked at the spongy gray object.

"It's a tongue!" Ben's nose crinkled up, but he poked it again.

"It's too big to be a tongue!" Joseph argued.

"No, trust me! We had an international food day at school last year. This one guy from some country, I don't remember which, brought cow tongue. It was so gross, and it looked just like this, only cooked," Ben explained, pleased he knew something his smart older brother didn't.

"Why would T. H. bring us a tongue?" Joseph looked at the bird as if it could answer him.

"Maybe . . ." Ben thought for a second, letting his imagination run wild, "maybe it's a bullfight. We have to fight a bull, like those guys with the red capes. It could be a bull tongue instead of a cow tongue. Maybe bulls are the enemy this time."

"Slow down!" Joseph laughed. "I don't think it's a bullfight. Where in the world do you come up with this stuff?"

They sat for a minute, looking at the tongue, trying to guess what the quest was. Ben broke the silence with a silly grin on his face.

"I feel sorry for the cow that belonged to this tongue. She must not be able to talk anymore." Ben laughed, and Joseph cracked up.

"If she was anything like you, I'm sure her family's happy she can't talk," Joseph teased.

"Hey! I don't talk *that* much!" Ben grinned.

Without any warning, True Heart swooped down and pecked at the tongue. He ripped a huge piece out of it and tilted his head. Both boys gasped.

"If he's going to do what I think he's going to do—" Joseph started.

True Heart gulped several times, and the chunk of tongue slid slowly down his throat.

"Eww! That is so gross, T. H.!" Joseph gagged. Ben just laughed. True Heart gave them an innocent look.

6

CLUES IN THE DIRT

By Saturday Ben and Joseph still didn't know what the clues meant, and nothing else had happened with the quest. Mom had decided that Saturdays were now gardening days. No matter how much the boys griped and complained during breakfast, she scooted them out the backdoor to start weeding as soon as they had eaten. At ten o'clock Sam showed up, and their parents left to do some shopping.

Kneeling in the dirt, Joseph wiped the

sweat off his face. He couldn't believe it was so hot this early in the morning.

Ben sat back on his heels and sighed. His sister stood nearby, her big, curious eyes watching them weed. Ben looked jealously at the Popsicle in Katie's little hands. Green sticky juice dripped all over her fingers, around her mouth, and down the front of her shirt. When Ben went back to work, True Heart fluttered down and landed in the dirt.

Katie was the only one who noticed as the falcon scratched in the dirt at the side of the garden. The curious little girl walked closer to see what True Heart was doing.

"Birdie drew A," Katie announced. "A, B, C, D, E, F . . ." She started to sing the alphabet song. It was one of her favorites, and she sang it so often it drove the boys crazy. Joseph and Ben looked over at her and then down at the dirt where she pointed.

"Hey, did you draw this, Katie?" Ben asked.

"No, T. T. did." Katie stopped singing for a second and then started up again.

"I told you a hundred times already. It's T. H.!" Joseph grumbled, but he didn't really mind.

"T. H. drew this letter A. Are you kidding?" Ben retraced the letter in the dirt. "We have the smartest bird in the world! He knows his alphabet!"

"That's pretty amazing. I bet it's the third clue," Joseph suggested.

Now that they had seen his drawing, True Heart started digging in the same spot again. He dug a little deeper and came up with a dull plastic medal on a faded blue-and-white striped ribbon, the kind of thing you get at a little kid's birthday party. True Heart offered it to Katie. She took the dirty plastic medal and put it around her neck.

"I winner! Ta-da! Clap, Ben! Clap, Joseph!" she commanded. They laughed and gave her the applause she wanted, and then they sat back, confused. Katie continued to strut around, proudly wearing the medal and singing her ABCs.

"What does all this mean?" Ben moaned, clutching his head and shaking it.

"Maybe we should ask Sam. She's a knight now, too. Maybe she could help," Joseph said.

Ben agreed, and they tramped into the house where Sam was in the kitchen washing the breakfast dishes.

"We need your help," Ben announced. She turned around with a soapy plate held out in front of her.

"This sounds serious," she smiled. "Okay, shoot."

"The first clue was a rattlesnake, but don't worry, T. H. didn't let go of it," Joseph assured her when a look of horror crossed her face. "The next clue was a cow's tongue," he explained. Then he told her about the letter A and the medal. She dried the plate and set it in the cupboard, all the while thinking hard about what they'd told her.

"Well, sometimes in old books they call someone who lies a 'serpent's tongue.' Maybe that has something to do with the snake and the tongue. But I have no idea about the other clues," Sam said after she'd finished a couple more dishes.

"Thanks, Sam!" Ben said eagerly. "Maybe we have to beware of bad guys who lie. At least we have something to go on now."

"No problem," Sam said. "How about driving to the store for some ice cream bars? You boys have been working pretty hard."

They cheered, and Joseph ran to get Sam's car keys for her.

7

A REAL TEST IN MATH

Joseph's seventh-grade math teacher moved up and down the aisle, passing out tests. "I want you all to show your work. Use pencils—no calculators—and good luck. Just remember what we've learned in this chapter, and you'll be fine."

Joseph shuffled his feet back and forth anxiously. He hadn't studied as much as he should have because he had been too busy thinking about the quest. But he was good at math and had finished all his homework. He hoped that would be enough.

Everyone was working quietly on the test when the principal walked in.

"Ms. Smith, can I talk to you?"

The principal sounded serious. It was more like a command than a question. Ms. Smith followed Principal Murphy into the hall.

When the teacher was gone, several boys decided to use the time to their advantage.

"Hey, Joseph, buddy! What's the answer to number three?" one rather large, strong-looking boy asked.

"I need number six!" another of the boys piped in.

Joseph looked up. These boys weren't his friends. They were the school bully and his posse.

"Do your own work, Henry," Joseph mumbled.

The large boy looked shocked. "Excuse me? Did you just say what I think you said? Let me see your answers, nerd, or else," Henry commanded.

Joseph shook his head, and Henry's face turned almost purple in anger.

"You'll be sorry, punk," Henry hissed. "David," he commanded another boy, "read the answers from the book on Ms. Smith's desk."

The frightened boy hurried to the front of the room and opened the answer book. He kept glancing worriedly at the door as he flipped through the book to find the right page.

"Tell us number fifteen, Baby Davy, before you wet your pants," Henry taunted.

David read off number fifteen, shut the book, and hurried back to his seat.

Joseph kept his head down, but his heart was pounding. Number fifteen was worth twenty points. It was a huge story problem, and he hadn't been able to figure it out yet. Without a correct answer on that problem, he wouldn't be able to get an A on the test. Would it be that bad just to write in the answer? He hadn't been the one who looked in the book. David had done it.

It wasn't his fault that everyone else was dishonest. He knew the rest of the class was writing in the answer. Joseph didn't want to look stupid and be the only one who missed that problem.

The door opened, and Ms. Smith walked back in. Everyone looked at their tests,

pretending that nothing had happened. Joseph suddenly remembered the quest. Was this his real test?

"Finish your tests quickly," Ms. Smith said. Joseph stood up and walked nervously to the front of the room. He placed his test with number fifteen left blank in the basket on Ms. Smith's desk.

"Ms. Smith, could I talk to you after class?" he asked quietly.

When Joseph returned to his seat, Henry was staring at him. "You better watch yourself, Joseph," Henry spat out in a whisper. "Trust me. Ms. Smith won't be able to protect you from my revenge."

Joseph waited for class to end and then stayed behind to explain to Ms. Smith what had happened while she was out of the room.

The rest of the day he felt jumpy and scared, wondering when Henry would get his revenge. Joseph had just started to walk home at the end of the day when suddenly Henry stepped out from behind a tree.

"Henry!" Joseph gasped.

Without a word, Henry punched him in the face, and Joseph fell to the sidewalk, landing on his hands. He looked at his scraped palms and winced. Luckily his nose didn't seem to be bleeding—yet.

"Here's for math today, nerd." Henry pulled back his foot. Joseph curled into a ball to protect himself.

Just then there was a loud snapping noise. As Henry's foot swung toward Joseph's stomach, Henry was the one who cried out in pain.

Joseph looked up, confused. Then a huge grin crossed his face. Henry had kicked an invisible metal coat. At least, it was invisible to Henry. Joseph could see it, and it was made of sparkling silver chain mail. He had earned his next piece of armor!

Henry looked completely confused. He kicked cautiously at Joseph again, swore, shook his head, and then turned and limped off in the other direction. Joseph hoped Henry's foot wasn't broken, but he couldn't help laughing out loud as he touched the metal coat with his fingertips.

8

BECOMING A WINNER

Ben sat in the gym with the rest of the eager fifth-graders, watching the school-wide fitness competition. The last event was the rope climb. This was Ben's event. A rope tied to the top of the high ceiling dangled down to touch the ground. The contestants were judged on how fast they could climb the rope and touch the ceiling to stop the clock.

Most of the kids in the younger grades didn't get more than a hop off the floor, but a fourth-grader completed the climb in pretty good time. Still, Ben wasn't worried. At his last school, where he'd attended before his family moved, he had set the school record for the rope climb.

He wiped his sweaty hands on his gym shorts and stepped forward. His whole grade cheered him on, and his best friend, Tony, yelled extra loud.

Duke pushed forward to the front of the group and smirked. "Good luck, loser!" Duke called out.

Ben gave a confident wave at the bully as he approached the rope.

"Call out 'done' when you touch the ceiling," Coach instructed. "On your mark, get set, go!"

Ben scrambled up the rope like a monkey. He heard the cheering and the gasps of approval and knew he was doing well. The coach started counting loudly as the time approached the school record.

"Done!" Ben shouted. The fifth-graders cheered as Ben scurried back down. They surrounded him and congratulated him.

"You beat the school record! There is no way anyone will beat that time!" Tony clapped him on the back. "You're the best, Ben!"

"Thanks, Tony," Ben smiled nervously. They watched the last boy hurry up the rope, but he was two and a half seconds slower than Ben.

"And the winner of the rope climb is our new fifth-grade student, Ben Adams. His score on the rope climb put the fifth grade in first place over the sixth grade this year," the principal announced over the microphone. The fifth-graders chanted Ben's name as he climbed down the bleachers to accept the school fitness trophy. At the table, the judges congratulated him and handed him the silver cup that would stay in the fifth-grade class-room all year. The fifth-graders cheered loudly and crowded around him, giving each other high fives while admiring the trophy.

Ben looked at the trophy with a sick feeling in his stomach. He knew he hadn't touched the ceiling. He had been so worried he wouldn't win that he had called out "Done" too soon.

He knew what he had to do.

Pushing his way through the crowd, Ben walked back to the table and pushed the tro-phy back in front of one of the judges. She looked confused until he explained. "I didn't really touch the ceiling in the rope climb. I'm sorry I lied."

Instead of getting mad, the judge smiled gratefully. "Thank you for telling the truth. I'm proud of your integrity."

Ben didn't know what "integrity" meant but figured it must have something to do with being honest. He was just glad she wasn't angry.

"It looks like the sixth-graders have won the school-wide fitness contest after all," the announcer said as Ben walked back to his seat. The fifth-graders groaned in disappointment and stared angrily at him. Ben was embarrassed, but at least he didn't feel ashamed of himself anymore.

The rest of the day, Ben felt like he had a terrible disease because all the other kids

stayed away from him. He could hear them whispering and see them pointing whenever he walked by. Ben thought the day would never end.

School was almost over when the principal called Ben into his office. He praised Ben for his actions and proudly gave him a T-shirt that read "Carson Elementary Winner!"

"You really are a winner because of your honesty," the principal beamed. Ben looked at the T-shirt with its big letters and tried not to groan. There was no way he could wear this at school. No one else thought he was a winner.

"Go ahead, put it on! I want all your class-mates to see it!" the principal encouraged.

Ben changed into the shirt and mumbled "Thanks" as he turned to go. The principal patted him on the back and watched as he left the school.

Ben wanted to get home as fast as he could without anyone seeing him. He looked back at the principal standing at the window and started to jog. He ran past the crossing guard and down the street toward his house. He had just turned the corner and was looking behind him when he nearly ran into a group of four boys in the middle of the sidewalk.

"Well, look what Ben's wearing!" Duke said to his buddies. "Isn't that cute?"

Ben glanced up and down the street, hoping someone was around to help him, but no one was there. Duke's friends laughed as Duke pulled out a pocketknife and opened the blade.

"What are you doing?" Ben asked, backing away from the knife in horror.

"You're not a winner!" Duke said with disgust. "Hold him down for me, guys." Ben struggled against the hands that grabbed him, but he was no match for the three bigger boys. They pushed him to the ground and held his arms while Duke knelt on the ground next to him. Ben's heart pounded as the hand holding the knife moved closer to his chest.

"Help!" Ben yelled. "Somebody help me! T. H.! Joseph!"

"Shut up!" said Duke. "I'm not going to hurt poor little Ben! Of course, Principal Davis might hurt you when he sees his precious shirt with a hole in it." Duke grabbed the front of Ben's shirt. "It just ain't right to leave this 'winner' here."

As the knife touched his T-shirt, Ben heard a snapping noise. The blade didn't pierce the fabric but hit something metal instead. Duke frowned in confusion.

Ben opened his eyes and saw the shining silver chain mail. He felt like shouting with excitement—he'd passed the test!

9

EARNING THE TRUST OF THE KING

The boys followed True Heart as fast as they could to the castle. Their silver coats clinked as they ran, but the metal chain mail didn't slow them down. It felt surprisingly light and more comfortable than they had expected. They were eager to see King Arthur and tell him everything that had happened. In the throne room, Ben raced Joseph to where Arthur was sitting.

"I know what the test was this time!" he said as he came to a sudden stop in front of the throne.

"Me, too! It was being honest!" Joseph came up beside Ben.

"And not lying!" Ben added.

"You did very well. It was not an easy quest. Liars often justify their behavior by thinking that no one will ever know. But the important thing is that *you* would know. I needed to test your honesty to know if I could trust you. It is one of the most important requirements to be a Knight of the Round Table." The king smiled. "Can you tell me what the clues meant?"

"I know what the A was! I didn't cheat to get an A grade even though everyone else did," Joseph answered.

"And the medal was like the trophy! I couldn't lie about winning it," Ben added.

"Very good!" King Arthur praised. "What about the snake and the tongue?"

"You use your tongue to lie," Joseph guessed, and King Arthur nodded. "Sam said that liars were sometimes called 'serpent's tongue' or something like that."

"That is true. Lady Samantha is very bright, as are you. Do you know the answer to the question I asked you the last time you were here?"

Ben shook his head, trying to remember the question, but Joseph nodded excitedly and raised his hand. Then he pulled his hand down before Ben could tease him.

"Yes, young Joseph. What is the answer?"

"The knight wouldn't have taken the treasure from Mintara because he gave his word that he would take only the shield.

Even though the dragon was dead, he was honest and didn't go back on his word," Joseph answered.

"Oh! I knew that!" Ben slapped himself on the forehead. Joseph and King Arthur laughed.

"I want you to know, my young friends, I would give up my life before I betrayed my integrity. You can trust me to keep my word no matter what," King Arthur said soberly.

"We'll remember that. Thank you, Your Majesty!" Ben said sincerely.

"True Heart will lead you back," King Arthur concluded as the boys turned to go. When they reached the doors of the castle, they could hear King Arthur behind them. "Don't forget that right makes might, my boys. Right makes might."

10

A BRAVE YOUNG KNIGHT

Ben and Joseph walked across the draw-bridge, crossed the moat, and ran into the woods. They forgot to wait for T. H. to appear and give the all-clear signal. They were talking back and forth so excitedly they weren't watching the woods around them. Suddenly, something grabbed them from behind. Two huge hands held their shirts and picked them up. Joseph's shield clattered uselessly to the dirt, which seemed surprisingly far below him. Joseph thrashed his feet and arms and looked at his shield longingly, although he didn't know what good it would do right now.

The boys looked in fear at each other for a moment before turning their heads to look behind them. A huge grinning face with two large tusks curling out of its mouth looked back at them. Whatever the thing was, it wasn't human. With the horns on the top of its head, it looked more like a troll from a fairy tale than anything else.

"Hey, careful with the chain mail!" Ben griped, but his voice was a little shaky. "I just earned it today."

"I don't think he can understand you. He doesn't look very smart," Joseph told Ben.

The troll roared, covering them in troll spit.

"He just drooled all over us!" Ben groaned.

"What kind of monster drools on people like a baby?"

The troll growled again, and this time it sounded angrier.

"You're making things worse, Ben," Joseph whispered. "You need to be quiet."

The troll growled louder as if he agreed with Joseph, and then he butted his head into Ben's back. Joseph screamed as he saw the troll's tusks stuck in Ben's shoulder. Ben looked back in horror until the troll pulled away. The tusks had gotten tangled in Ben's chain mail. They hadn't penetrated his skin!

"That was close," whispered Ben. He wasn't joking now, and he looked at his older brother with fear in his eyes. "Joseph, what are we going to do?"

Then the boys heard True Heart screeching

from a tree further down the path. As they looked toward the falcon, Sam appeared on the path in front of the troll.

"Sam!" Joseph yelled. "Get out of here. Go get King Arthur."

Sam spun in a circle, searching frantically for somewhere to run for help.

Joseph realized that Sam didn't know how to get to the castle, and the hope he had felt at seeing her disappeared.

"Go for her!" Ben called loudly to the troll, pointing at Sam. "Girls taste better than boys! Promise! We taste awful! Go for her!"

The troll hesitated, grunting. Then he dropped the boys and ran for Sam.

Sam grabbed a huge rock, throwing it as hard as she could at the troll. The rock missed and fell to the ground, but it stopped

the troll in his tracks. Sam threw another
rock, and the troll looked at the ground,
puzzled. He seemed shocked that not only
were the boys gone but someone was throwing things at him. He picked up one of the
rocks Sam had thrown and threw it back.
Luckily, the troll didn't have any better aim
than Sam did. Sam threw another rock, and

then the troll threw a rock. It was like the troll thought they were playing a game. The boys inched closer to Sam, trying not to attract the troll's attention.

They had almost reached her when a rock hit Sam. Blood streamed from a cut on her arm. "Game over!" Sam yelled. She lifted a huge stone and hurled it as hard as she could

at the troll. This time the rock hit the troll on the side of his head with a loud thump. There was silence for a moment. Then the troll bellowed in pain and lumbered back into the woods.

Ben cheered. He ran to Sam and pulled her back into the trees while Joseph grabbed his shield and followed them.

"Girls taste better than boys? Go for her?" Sam asked angrily. "What was that about?"

"Um . . . it was just part of the bigger plan. I wasn't really going to let him eat you!" Ben said, sounding a little nervous. Sam rolled her eyes. Then she grabbed Joseph and Ben and hugged them, getting blood on Joseph's cheek and in Ben's hair.

"Sam, what were you doing out in the woods?" Ben asked.

"Not that we aren't happy to see you. You saved us," Joseph said before she could answer.

"Your parents got home, and you weren't back from the castle. I said I thought I knew where you were, and T. H. led me through the woods. I don't know about this knight thing, guys. You didn't tell me the Black Knight had friends. We were in serious danger back there. What are we going to tell your parents?"

"You'll think of something," Ben offered helpfully. "You were awesome. That troll was so scared! He's probably never had to face someone as brave as you!"

"Sam, we can't give up now. King Arthur needs us," Joseph said with concern.

"We'll see," said Sam.

They followed True Heart in silence the rest of the way home.

"Where were you? We've been so worried," their mother said as she hugged them both.

"Okay, okay! Enough mushy stuff already!" Ben groaned. Mom laughed and grabbed Ben's face to kiss him.

"Moms can do as much mushy stuff as they want, mister!" Then Mom saw the blood. "Ben, you're bleeding. What happened?"

"It's okay, Mom. It's just Sam's blood."

"Just Sam's blood?" Mom gasped. "Samantha! Oh, my goodness, what happened to your arm?"

Dad grabbed a towel, and Mom ushered Sam to the sink. Sam, Joseph, and Ben looked at each other.

"Mr. and Mrs. Adams, as soon as I get a

bandage on my arm, I'll tell you everything, I promise," Sam said.

The next thing Joseph and Ben knew, Sam's cut couldn't be seen. There was a loud snap, and her arm was protected by a shiny silver coat of chain mail.

Sam looked at the boys and smiled. Then she turned to their parents.

"Mr. and Mrs. Adams," she began, "Do you believe in King Arthur?"

Okay, Knights of Right, let's see if you've earned your armor. King Arthur has a few questions for you . . .

1. Why do you think King Arthur wants to know if Ben, Joseph, and Sam tell the truth?

2. What would you have done if you'd been Joseph in the math classroom?

3. Is it okay to let other people copy your answers in class? Why is it important not to cheat in school?

4. What would you have done if you'd been Ben climbing the rope and you knew you hadn't touched the ceiling?

5. At the end of the book, what would you have done if you'd been Sam ? Were you surprised when Sam told Ben and Joseph's parents the truth about how she had been hurt?

6. What do you think Ben and Joseph's parents will do now?

7. What are some of the consequences when you tell the truth? How do you feel about people who tell lies? How do you feel after you have told the truth, especially if you've been worried about the consequences?

8. Why is it sometimes hard to tell the truth?

King Arthur asks—Did you know?

1. Chronic and habitual liars rarely feel good about themselves (see http://www.myoutofcontrolteen.com/lying.html).

2. "Cheating prevents learning and masks true accomplishments and weakness" (Nancy Cole, quoted in "Teaching and Learning," *Education Week,* October 6, 1999; available at http://www.edweek.org/ew/articles/1999/10/06/06tl.h19.html).

3. Those with friends who have cheated are more apt to cheat themselves (ABCNews *Primetime* Poll: "Cheating among Teens Common, Effective," April 2005, http://abcnews.go.com/sections/primetime/US/cheating_poll_040429.html).

4. Children may lie to keep their parents or teachers happy. Parents need to show that they value the truth much more than an act of misbehavior (see http://www.myoutofcontrolteen.com/lying.html).

**Remember, Knights, right makes might.
Keep making good choices and
earning your armor!**

King Arthur

ABOUT THE AUTHOR

M'Lin Rowley is seventeen years old and attends American Fork High School in Utah, where her mascot is a caveman rather than a knight. She loves snow skiing, rock climbing, going to movies with her friends, and writing stories. M'Lin hopes that people will enjoy her books and learn something from them. *The Silver Coat,* book 2 of the Knights of Right series, is her second novel.